Helena
the Horse-riding
Fairy

For Aphra O'Brien
with lots of love

Special thanks to
Sue Mongredien

ISBN 978-0-545-20252-7

12 11 10 9 8 7 6 5 4 3 2   10 11 12 13 14 15/0

Printed in the U.S.A.   40

First Scholastic Printing, April 2010

Helena
the Horse-riding Fairy

by Daisy Meadows

SCHOLASTIC INC.

New York Toronto London Auckland
Sydney Mexico City New Delhi Hong Kong

The Fairyland Palace

Fairyla

Parking Lot

Buses

Riding Stables

Cooke Soccer Stadium

Basketball Courts

Soccer Fields

Tippington Town

REC CENTER

Swimming Pool

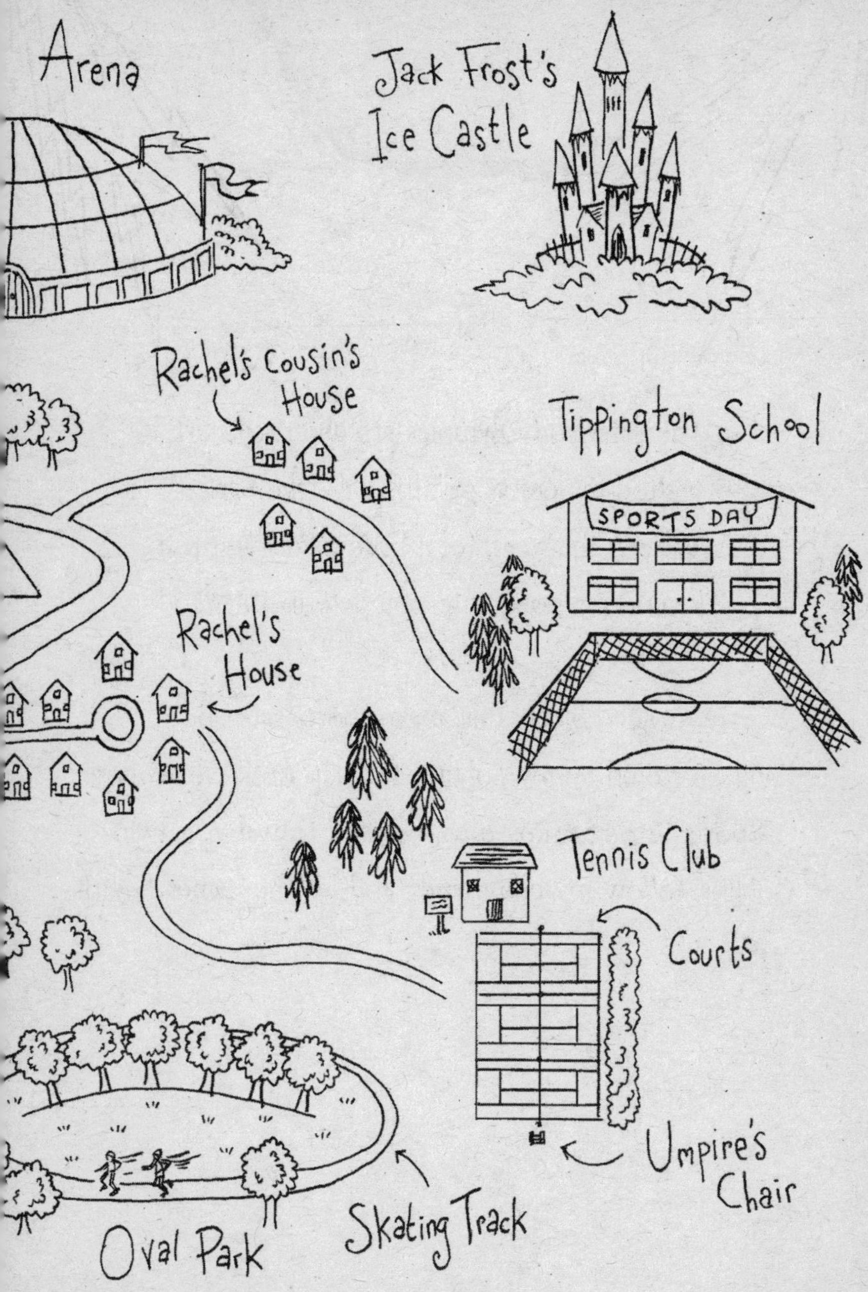

Arena

Jack Frost's
Ice Castle

Rachel's Cousin's
House

Tippington School

SPORTS DAY

Rachel's
House

Tennis Club

Courts

Umpire's
Chair

Oval Park

Skating Track

The Fairyland Olympics are about to start,
And my crafty goblins will take part.
We'll win this year, for I have a cunning plan.
I'll send my goblins to compete in Fairyland.

The magic objects that make sports safe and fun
Will be stolen by my goblins, to keep until we've won.
Sports Fairies, prepare to lose and to watch us win.
Goblins, follow my commands, and let the games begin!

Contents

Magic Message

"There," Rachel Walker said, pulling back her hair. "I'm ready. Are you?"

Kirsty Tate buttoned her riding pants and smiled at her best friend. "Yes," she said. "I can't wait!"

It was the first day of the spring vacation, and Kirsty had come to stay with Rachel's family for a week. In a few minutes, they would be heading out for a riding lesson at the Tippington Stables, and both girls were looking forward to it. They always seemed to have the most fun when they were together—and the most exciting adventures!

Kirsty was just about to open the door, when something caught her eye. Rachel's music box was open on her dresser, even though it had been closed just a minute before. "Rachel!" she said, pointing. "Look!"

She and Rachel ran over excitedly.
They had each been given matching
music boxes by the king and queen of
Fairyland, as thank-you presents for
helping the fairies. The two girls had been
friends with the fairies long enough to
know that the open, tinkling music box
could only mean one thing: Something
magical was about to happen!

Kirsty held her breath as she peeked
in the music box. She gasped when she
spotted a piece of paper tucked inside.
As the girls watched, sparkly gold
writing appeared on the paper, letter
by letter.

"It's a message," Rachel whispered,
her heart pounding.

We . . . need . . . your . . . help! the
golden letters spelled.

We need your help!

"The fairies must be in trouble!" Kirsty cried. "Do you think Jack Frost has been up to more mischief?"

"There's only one way to find out," Rachel said, and Kirsty nodded.

Both girls opened the golden lockets around their necks, and took out pinches of fairy dust.

"Let's go to Fairyland," said Kirsty, flinging the fairy dust over herself.

"To Fairyland!" Rachel echoed, doing the same. The two girls were immediately swept up in a magical whirlwind of rainbow-colored sparkles. As they were whisked away, they felt themselves shrinking to become fairy-size. Kirsty smiled as she glanced over her shoulder and saw a pair of delicate wings on her back, glittering with magic.

Seconds later, they were set down gently in Fairyland, in front of an unfamiliar building. It was very grand, with white marble walls and glittering golden pillars in the front.

King Oberon and Queen Titania stepped forward to greet the girls. Behind them were seven other fairies that Rachel and Kirsty didn't recognize.

"Thank you for coming," the king said.

"Yes, thank you," the queen

added. "We called you because our Sports Fairies really need your help." She gestured to the fairies who stood nearby. "This is Helena the Horse-riding Fairy, Stacey the Soccer Fairy, Zoe the Skating Fairy, Brittany the Basketball Fairy, Samantha the Swimming Fairy, Alice the Tennis Fairy, and Gemma the Gymnastics Fairy." Each fairy smiled and said hello, looking happy to see Rachel and Kirsty.

"Hello," Rachel said, curtsying to the king and queen and smiling at the Sports Fairies. Then she looked around curiously. "Um . . . where are we? I don't recognize this part of Fairyland."

"This is the Fairyland Arena," Helena explained, "where all the sporting events take place."

"Come and see," the queen said, waving at the golden doors. They swung open immediately, and Kirsty and Rachel followed the fairies through to a large stadium. There were rows of white seats surrounding a soccer field of the greenest grass the girls had ever seen.

"Wow," Kirsty breathed. "My dad would love this!"

"That's not all," Samantha told them. "If

we need to change it for a different sport,
we just do this . . ." She waved her wand
and a stream of sparkly fairy dust billowed
out. The soccer field gleamed bright gold,
and a rainbow-colored mist covered it.
Then the mist cleared, and where the
grass had been seconds before was now
a swimming pool! Its turquoise water
shimmered in the sunshine.

Rachel blinked. "That's amazing!" she
said with awe.

The queen smiled. "Our Sports Fairies help make sports fun and exciting, both in Fairyland and in the human world," she explained.

"And we also make sure sporting events run smoothly, and that everyone plays fairly," added Zoe.

"How do you do that?" Kirsty asked.

"With our magic objects," Stacey

told her. "I have a magic soccer ball, Samantha has magic goggles, Alice has a magic tennis racket . . ."

"Not anymore, though," Alice added sadly. "Because our magic objects have been stolen!"

Burglars Break In!

"Stolen?" echoed Kirsty. "What happened?"

"Well," Brittany began, "when we're not using our magic objects, we keep them in our lockers here at the arena. But when we came to pick them up this morning, the lockers were empty!"

"So who could have taken them?" Rachel asked. Then she sighed.

She already knew the answer.

Gemma nodded, as if reading Rachel's mind. "Yes," she said. "Jack Frost and his goblins. We have special keys that open our lockers." She showed the girls a tiny bow-shaped key that she wore on a silver chain around her neck. "We think that Jack Frost used his special ice magic to make copies of them."

"Then he sent his goblins to break into our lockers and steal our magic objects," Zoe went on.

"Let's go to the seeing pool," Queen

Titania suggested. "Then we can watch
how it happened." She waved her
wand. They were all whisked up
in a sparkly magical whirlwind
that took them to the
edge of a clear blue
pool in the palace
garden. The queen
waved her wand
once more, and the
pool rippled with
color.

The girls watched as images appeared
on the water. They could see the seven
Sports Fairies flying toward the arena at
dawn, the sun painting the sky orange
and red. Down below were several
goblins. One stumbled as he kicked a

soccer ball; two others tried to pass a
basketball to each other, but missed
every time; and others fell over as they
practiced handstands and cartwheels.
Kirsty and Rachel watched as the Sports
Fairies flew down toward the goblins.

"We always try to help if someone is struggling at a sport," Stacey explained.

"But it was all a trick." Gemma sighed. "The goblins were just trying to distract us, and keep us away from the locker room!"

The water in the pool rippled and the image changed again. Now Rachel and Kirsty could see seven goblins, dressed in black with ski masks on their heads. They were climbing up the arena wall with a rope. They kept slipping and stepping on one another but, eventually,

they all scrambled into the arena
through the window.

"That's the window of the locker room,"
Samantha told the girls. "*Our* locker
room!"

Once inside, the tallest goblin shouted,
"Get the ice keys ready!" Each goblin
took an icy key from his pocket and tried
it in the locker in
front of him.

There was all
kinds of confusion
at first. None of
the goblins could
find the lock that
matched his key, but they finally figured
it out.

As the last key went in, all seven doors
opened, revealing the magic objects inside:

a riding helmet, a soccer ball, a skate lace,
a basketball, swim goggles, a tennis racket,
and a hoop—all sparkling with fairy
magic.

Each goblin eagerly grabbed one of the
magic objects.

"Now, remember what Jack Frost told
us," the tallest goblin said. "If we're going
to win the Fairyland Olympics, we need
to practice our sports with the other

goblins. But make sure you keep the
magic objects hidden while you practice
in the human world. We don't want the
fairies to find them! Then, in a week, we'll
come back to Fairyland . . . and win the
Olympics!"

The other goblins cheered, and they
all sprinted back
to the window.
Rachel couldn't help
noticing how much
more athletic they
seemed now that
they had the Sports
Fairies' magic objects. The goblin with the
gymnastics hoop even did a series of back
handsprings across the floor!

Then the scene in the pool faded, and
the water became clear again.

"The Fairyland Olympics start in seven days," King Oberon explained. "Jack Frost knows that when the magic objects are away from the Sports Fairies or their lockers, sporting events will be ruined everywhere. Nobody will be able to enjoy sports like they usually do."

The queen nodded. "He also knows that the magic objects are so powerful that they make anyone near them perform very well at sports," she added. "He wants his goblins to win the Olympics, so that he can get his hands on the prize."

"What is the prize?" Kirsty asked.

"The Fairyland Olympics Cup," the queen replied. "It's filled with luck—which would

mean Jack Frost could get away with all kinds of new mischief!"

"Can the Olympics be postponed until the magic objects are found?" Rachel suggested.

"No." The king sighed. "The Fairyland Olympics are linked to the human Olympics. If we postpone our Olympics, it would cause tremendous troubles for the ones in your world."

"That's right," Zoe said. "But as long as our magical objects are missing, nobody will be able to play well."

"Nobody will enjoy sports very much, either," Stacey added.

"We've just got to get our objects back," Brittany cried. "Otherwise both of the Olympic Games, and all sports, will be ruined!"

Girls on the Case

"We'll help you in any way we can," Rachel said at once.

"Thank you," Helena replied gratefully. "We know the goblins will be practicing their new skills, so they'll probably turn up in places connected with each magic object."

"We're going riding today," Kirsty

remembered. "Maybe the goblin with your magic riding helmet will be there, Helena." In her green riding jacket, tan riding pants, and boots, Kirsty thought Helena was dressed perfectly for riding—except that she was missing

the special riding helmet that all riders need! Helena looked excited. "I'll come with you in case he is," she said. "Let's go back to your world right away!"

The girls had just enough time to say good-bye to the fairies before Helena waved her wand and whisked them away to Rachel's room. The girls turned

back to their normal sizes once more.

"Are you ready, girls?" they heard
Mr. Walker calling.

Helena tucked herself into Kirsty's pocket
as the girls hurried downstairs. Rachel's dad
was waiting to drive them to the stables.
Both girls felt tingly with excitement as
they got into the car. It was wonderful to be
starting a new fairy adventure!

It was only a short ride to Tippington Stables, and soon Mr. Walker was parking the car.

"Have fun," he told the girls as they jumped out. "I'll come and pick you up at the end of your lesson."

"Bye, Dad!" Rachel called. She turned to Kirsty. "Our instructor is named Vivian," she said. "Let's go and find her."

As the girls walked toward the stables,

Helena peeked out of Kirsty's pocket. "I can sense a lot of confusion here," she said anxiously. "I wonder what's going on."

Rachel and Kirsty walked around to the riding ring and stared in horror at the chaos that greeted them. Horses and ponies were trotting back and forth without riders, and the stable hands were running around trying to catch them. One girl was attempting to mount, but the girth on her pony hadn't been tightened. The saddle slipped, dumping the rider straight onto the ground.

Kirsty helped the girl to her feet.

Luckily she was unhurt. She quickly
thanked Kirsty before going back to her
horse.

A lady with red hair hurried over,
and Helena ducked into Kirsty's pocket
again.

"Hi, Vivian," Rachel said to the red-
haired lady. "Is everything all right?"

Vivian sighed. "I'm afraid it's kind of

hectic today, girls!" she said. "I'm trying to sort everything out before your lesson. You're going to ride Shadow, Rachel, and your friend will be on Brandy. Why don't you go and tack up? I'll be with you as soon as I have everything under control."

"OK," Rachel said, as she and Kirsty headed off to find their ponies. They'd hardly taken a step when a rider went trotting past—facing backward on her pony!

"Oh no!" Vivian cried, rushing to help.

"I'll meet you in the ring, girls!" she
called over her shoulder.

Helena peeked out again. "This is

awful," she said, looking worried as
she peered around the stables. "And it's
all because my magic riding helmet is
missing. If I had that, then none of this
would be happening!" Suddenly she
frowned, deep in concentration. Then her
tiny face brightened. "It's here," she said.

"My magic riding helmet is here—I can sense it." She stared in dismay as another horse trotted past without a rider on its back. "But we've got to find it soon," she added, "before things get any worse!"

A Sweet Idea

Rachel and Kirsty went to tack up,
keeping an eye out for any goblins
that might have Helena's magic riding
helmet.

"Good boy, Brandy," Kirsty said,
patting her toffee-colored pony as she
adjusted her stirrups. Brandy tossed his
head impatiently as Kirsty attempted

to get the stirrups even, but one of
the stirrup leathers just wouldn't go
any shorter.

"Ah!" said Helena, flying onto Kirsty's
shoulder. "It's only because my helmet
is missing that you're having this much
trouble, but I know a trick that might
help. If you twist the strap around the
stirrup, it'll make it a little shorter.
Watch!" Helena waved her wand. Kirsty
watched with delight as the
stirrup leather came
undone, looped itself
through the stirrup,
and then buckled
itself again,
making the
stirrups perfectly
even.

"Thank you, Helena!" Kirsty smiled.

Meanwhile, Rachel was having trouble getting Shadow to take the bit in his mouth.

"Everything's more difficult because my helmet's missing." Helena sighed. "Let me try, Rachel." She hovered close to Shadow's left ear and spoke gently to him. Rachel couldn't hear what she said, but Shadow was suddenly happy to take the bit.

"Thanks," Rachel said gratefully. "Vivian said we should meet her in the ring, didn't she? Let's go over there now."

The girls led their ponies through the stable yard and out to the riding ring. When they arrived, they were surprised to see that a boy on a gray horse was already there. He was cantering in a circle, riding confidently. He was having much more success than anyone else they'd seen that day!

The girls stopped and watched closely. As the gray horse jumped over

a fence, the boy's helmet lifted up ever
so slightly. Kirsty
gasped. The boy had
a pointy green nose!

"He's a goblin!"
she whispered
to Rachel and
Helena.

"And he's
wearing my
helmet!" Helena
exclaimed, annoyed.

Rachel frowned. "But it's so big,"
she said. "The helmet, I mean. I was
expecting it to be the same size as
it was in Fairyland."

"Oh no," Helena said. "Our magic
objects adjust their size to fit whoever is
holding them."

"So how are we going to get it back?"
Kirsty wondered aloud. "If the goblin
sees us coming after his helmet, he'll just
ride away."

Rachel thought hard. "Helena, what
do horses like to eat more than anything
else?" she asked.

"Most horses love sugar cubes," the
little fairy replied. "Why?"

Rachel smiled.
"Could you use your
magic to conjure
some?" she asked.
Helena nodded. "Of
course," she said, waving
her wand. Immediately,
a pile of sparkling white
sugar cubes appeared in Rachel's hand.

"Great!" Rachel declared. "Now,

how about we try
tempting that horse
over to us with a
trail of sugar cubes?
Then we might be
able to persuade the goblin to give us
back the helmet!"

"Good idea," said Kirsty.

Helena waved her wand again, and
a flurry of horseshoe-shaped fairy dust
swirled all around the pile of sugar cubes.
One by one, the cubes jumped down
from Rachel's hand and started bouncing
along the grass, lining up to make a trail
from the girls toward the goblin's horse.

It didn't take long for the gray horse
to notice the sugar cubes. She had been
cantering but, at the sight of her favorite
treat, she slowed down. She immediately

dropped her head to eat one of the cubes.

The goblin seemed a little confused by the appearance of the sugar, and he looked around. Then he noticed the girls in the corner of the riding ring, and frowned. "What are you doing here?" he asked. A suspicious look came over his face and he touched the helmet protectively. "Hey — you haven't seen any fairies around here, have you?"

Rachel and Kirsty exchanged glances and gulped. How were they going to answer that question truthfully ... without scaring the goblin away?

A Ride to the Rescue

Rachel thought quickly. "Fairies? I
don't see any fairies," she replied. It was
true—since Helena was now hiding at
the bottom of Kirsty's pocket.

"That helmet you're wearing . . ." Kirsty
said to the goblin as the gray horse came
closer, eating the next lump of sugar in
the line. "It's not yours, is it?"

The goblin gave a clever grin. "No, but I'm keeping it," he told her, and winked. "This helmet is going to help my team win at the Fairyland Olympics!"

"But that would be cheating," Rachel said. "If you give it back to us, we can return it to its rightful owner."

The goblin cackled and shook his head. "No way," he said. "It's mine now. I'll show those fairies a thing or—Hey!" He broke off in surprise as Helena flew out

of Kirsty's pocket and zoomed toward
him with a determined look on her face.
"Yikes! What are you doing?" the goblin
cried as she flew toward the riding helmet.
She pulled on it with her tiny hands, but,
unfortunately, she was too small. She
couldn't move it one bit.

"Oh no, you don't!" the goblin yelled.
He batted Helena away, and tugged on
his horse's reins. The horse cantered off,
leaving the fairy far behind.

"You can't catch me!" he yelled gleefully over his shoulder.

Rachel and Kirsty ran over to their own ponies, mounted them quickly, and directed them to chase after the goblin. Helena flew alongside them. "Try to stay as close to the goblin as you can," she encouraged. "As long as you're close to my magic riding helmet, its power will affect you, too, so you'll be able to ride well."

"OK," Kirsty replied, hunching lower over Brandy and urging him to go faster.

"But it works both ways," Helena added. "The farther you are from the helmet, the worse your riding will become."

"Come on, Shadow," Rachel urged. "Keep going!"

The girls gradually gained ground on the goblin and realized that Helena was

right. The closer they got to him, the
easier it was to ride.

The goblin glanced over his shoulder
and looked panicked to see how close
the girls were getting. He urged his horse
on and it broke into a gallop. His horse
quickly pulled away from Brandy and
Shadow.

As the gap widened, Kirsty could
feel her control slipping. Brandy

stumbled on a rough patch of grass,
and nervously slowed down.

Rachel was struggling to stay in her
saddle, too, but she knew they had
to get closer to the goblin's horse again.
"Come on, boy," she said encouragingly.
"You can do it!"

All three horses were now approaching
a tall hedge that bordered the pasture.
It was a huge
jump, but the
goblin's horse
didn't hesitate.
He took it
at full speed!
Thanks to the
magic of the
riding helmet,
the horse

cleared the hedge easily, leaving the girls
behind on the
other side.

With the tall
hedge now
between them,
the effect of the
magic riding
helmet wore off completely. Rachel
flopped around on Shadow's back, losing
her grip.

Kirsty was being jolted around, too. She
felt very frightened! She was getting closer
and closer to the hedge, which looked
more enormous by the second. She wasn't
sure that Brandy was going to be able to
jump high enough, especially not when
her riding skills seemed to have vanished.
She tried to think of a way to stop her

pony, but her mind was blank with fright.
She couldn't remember what to do!

Kirsty glanced over at Rachel,
wondering if her friend could help,
but Rachel looked just as terrified. She
was white-faced, clinging to Shadow
for dear life. Her pony thundered toward
the hedge.

Kirsty's hands were sweating. Suddenly,
the reins slipped from her grasp altogether.
"Help!" she cried, as she felt herself falling.

Helena Helps!

Just as Kirsty thought she was about to hit the ground, there was a flash of bright pink light in her eyes. She felt herself shrinking! Down, down, down she went, smaller and smaller, until she was a fairy with shining wings. She fluttered her wings thankfully and soared into the air.

Rachel did the same, and both girls flew gratefully over to Helena. "Thank you," gasped Rachel. "That was scary!"

Brandy and Shadow both jumped over the hedge without their riders, and then came to a stop in the next field. They put their heads down to graze.

Once they saw that
their ponies were safe,
the three fairies
zoomed after the
goblin. His horse
was still galloping.

"We've got to think of
a way to get that helmet
off his head," Rachel
said as they flew. "But how?"

"Helena, could your magic unsnap
the strap?" Kirsty wondered. Helena
nodded, and Kirsty pointed toward
a jump the goblin's horse was
approaching. "If we can catch up with
him in time, maybe you could magically
undo the chin strap just after the jump,"
she said. "Then, as his horse lands, the
helmet should fly off his head . . ."

"And we can catch it!" Rachel finished.

"It's a great idea," Helena said hopefully. "Let's do it!"

The three fairies flew toward the goblin. "Of course, once the helmet comes off his head, he won't be able to ride very well anymore," Helena murmured to herself. "I'll have to make sure he doesn't get hurt."

"He's coming up to the jump!" Rachel cried.

Helena pointed her wand at the magic riding helmet. As the gray horse rose to meet the fence, a swirling cloud of pink fairy dust fluttered in the air. When the goblin landed on the other side, the strap came loose—and the helmet tumbled right off the goblin's head!

As the helmet flew through the air,
Rachel and Kirsty darted for it and
caught the helmet between them.
Immediately, the helmet shimmered and
shrank down to Fairyland-size.

Meanwhile, the goblin had completely
lost control of his horse and had
bounced right out of the saddle!

"Whoaaaa!" he cried in alarm as he fell toward the ground.

But Helena skillfully flicked her wand at a nearby water trough. It flew through  the air and stopped just under the tumbling goblin. He fell into the water with a *splash*! Kirsty and Rachel couldn't help laughing. They knew goblins hated getting wet! "It serves him right for trying to cheat," Rachel said as the goblin climbed out of the trough, dripping wet.

"Maybe you should go back to Fairyland and dry off!" Helena called as he stomped off in a huff.

Kirsty and Rachel gave the magic

riding helmet to Helena, who popped it back on her head with a smile of relief.

"Thank you," she said, and touched it with her wand. There was a flash of twinkling pink lights all around the helmet.

"There," she said happily. "I've just set everything right. Horse riding is a lot more safe and fun again for everyone!"

"Hooray!" cheered Rachel and Kirsty.

Helena gave them both a hug, then waved her wand to turn them back to their normal sizes. "Thanks again, girls," she said. "I'll fly to Fairyland now and tell the others the good news!"

"Bye, Helena," Kirsty said. She waved

as she and Rachel
watched the little
fairy zoom away.
"Oh, girls, there
you are! And
you've found
Mischief. Thank you!" came
a voice. The girls looked up and saw
Vivian at the end of the field.

Rachel and Kirsty glanced at each other, realizing that Mischief must be the name of the gray horse the  goblin had been riding. "Yes, she was in the ring," Rachel said truthfully. "We followed her here."

Vivian looked very relieved. "Thank goodness," she said. "She must have gotten loose in all the craziness. Thank you, girls. I'll take her back to the barn, and then we can begin your lesson. I'm sorry for the slow start today, but everything seems to be back to normal now."

Kirsty and Rachel smiled at each other. They knew why everything was

back to normal. It was because Helena
the Horse-riding Fairy had her magic
riding helmet back again.

"That was exciting," Rachel said as
she mounted Shadow, noticing how
much easier it was this time.

Kirsty nodded. "Yes," she said. "Now we just have to find the other six magic objects in time for the Fairyland Olympics." She grinned. "I think this is going to be a *fairy* busy week!"

RAINBOW magic™

THE SPORTS FAIRIES

Now Rachel and Kirsty need to help

Stacey the Soccer Fairy!

Jack Frost's goblins have stolen Stacey's
magic soccer ball! Can Rachel and
Kirsty help her find it, or will the
Fairyland Olympics be ruined?

Join their next adventure
in this special sneak peek!

Soccer Superstars

"You look great, Dad!" Rachel Walker laughed, glancing at her father as she climbed out of the car. Mr. Walker was wearing a blue-and-white soccer jersey and scarf, his face was painted with blue and white stripes, and he had a fluffy blue-and-white wig on his head.

"The wig's fantastic!" Kirsty Tate, Rachel's best friend, added with a grin. She was staying with the Walkers over spring vacation. "He's going to be the best-dressed Tippington Rovers fan here."

Rachel nodded. "I'm glad Mom and I are just wearing scarves, though," she added. "That wig looks kind of warm!"

"It is, but I want to show my support for the team," said Mr. Walker, as they left the parking lot and joined the other soccer fans heading toward the Cooke Stadium. "This is a very important game, girls. If Tippington beats the Compton Capitals today, the team will be moved up to the next league!"

Rachel and Kirsty exchanged concerned glances. They were both worried that the soccer game would be a complete disaster, because the Sports Fairies had lost their magic objects! When these special objects were in their proper places — with the Sports Fairies or in the fairies' lockers — they ensured that sports in both the human and fairy worlds were safe, fun, and exciting. Unfortunately, the objects had been stolen by the mischievous Jack Frost and his goblins. . . .

RAINBOW magic™

There's Magic in Every Series!

The Rainbow Fairies

The Weather Fairies

The Jewel Fairies

The Pet Fairies

The Fun Day Fairies

The Petal Fairies

The Dance Fairies

The Music Fairies

The Sports Fairies

The Party Fairies

Read them all!

📖 **SCHOLASTIC**

www.scholastic.com

www.rainbowmagiconline.com

HIT entertainment

RMFAIRY2

RAINBOW magic™

SPECIAL EDITION

Three Books in One!
More Rainbow Magic Fun!

www.scholastic.com
www.rainbowmagiconline.com

HiT entertainment

RMSPECIAL2